KT-524-184

LAUGH YOUR SOCKS OFF with

Jeremy STRONG

Return of the Hundred Mile-An-Hour Dog

Illustrated by

Rowan Clifford

PUFFIN

PUFFIN BOOKS

Published by the Penguin Group
Penguin Books Ltd, 80 Strand, London WC2R ORL, England
Penguin Group (USA) Inc., 375 Hudson Street, New York, New York 10014, USA
Penguin Group (Canada), 90 Eglinton Avenue East, Suite 700, Toronto, Ontario, Canada M4P 2Y3
(a division of Pearson Penguin Canada Inc.)
Penguin Ireland, 25 St Stephen's Green, Dublin 2, Ireland (a division of Penguin Books Ltd)
Penguin Group (Australia), 250 Camberwell Road, Camberwell, Victoria 3124, Australia
(a division of Pearson Australia Group Pty Ltd)
Penguin Books India Pvt Ltd, 11 Community Centre, Panchsheel Park, New Delhi – 110 017, India
Penguin Group (NZ), 67 Apollo Drive, Mairangi Bay, Auckland 1310, New Zealand
(a division of Pearson New Zealand Ltd)
Penguin Books (South Africa) (Pty) Ltd, 24 Sturdee Avenue, Rosebank, Johannesburg 2196, South Africa

Penguin Books Ltd, Registered Offices: 80 Strand, London WC2R ORL, England

penguin.com

First published 2005
This edition published 2007

017

Text copyright © Jeremy Strong, 2005
Illustrations copyright © Rowan Clifford, 2005
All rights reserved

The moral right of the author and illustrator has been asserted

Set in Baskerville MT
Made and printed in England by Clays Ltd, St Ives plc

Except in the United States of America, this book is sold subject to the condition
that it shall not, by way of trade or otherwise, be lent, re-sold, hired out, or otherwise
circulated without the publisher's prior consent in any form of binding or cover other than
that in which it is published and without a similar condition including this condition
being imposed on the subsequent purchaser

British Library Cataloguing in Publication Data
A CIP catalogue record for this book is available from the British Library

ISBN: 978-0-141-32235-3

www.greenpenguin.co.uk

MIX
Paper from
responsible sources
FSC™ C018179
www.fsc.org

Penguin Books is committed to a sustainable
future for our business, our readers and our planet.
This book is made from Forest Stewardship
Council™ certified paper.

This is Trevor.
He's looking for his dog.

There she is!

No, she's
over there!

It's Streaker, the jet-propelled
hurricane.

Jeremy Strong once worked in a bakery, putting the jam into three thousand doughnuts every night. Now he puts the jam in stories instead, which he finds much more exciting. At the age of three, he fell out of a first-floor bedroom window and landed on his head. His mother says that this damaged him for the rest of his life and refuses to take any responsibility. He loves writing stories because he says it is 'the only time you alone have complete control and can make anything happen'. His ambition is to make you laugh (or at least snuffle). Jeremy Strong lives near Bath with four cats and a flying cow.

Read more about Streaker's adventures
THE HUNDRED-MILE-AN-HOUR DOG
RETURN OF THE HUNDRED-MILE-AN-HOUR DOG
WANTED! THE HUNDRED-MILE-AN-HOUR DOG

Are you feeling silly enough to read more?
MY DAD'S GOT AN ALLIGATOR!
MY GRANNY'S GREAT ESCAPE
MY MUM'S GOING TO EXPLODE!
MY BROTHER'S FAMOUS BOTTOM

BEWARE! KILLER TOMATOES
CHICKEN SCHOOL
KRAZY KOW SAVES THE WORLD – WELL, ALMOST

This is especially for Maria and Anna who, along with lots of others, wanted to know if Charlie Smugg ever got into the horse trough – and did Tina manage to get Trevor? Now you can all find out.

In memory of Molly and Mabel, who both died in 2003, and who were the original inspiration for Streaker.

Contents

1 Four-Legged Asteroids and Wet Dishcloths

It wasn't my idea. It was Tina's, and don't go thinking 'Ooh, Trevor's got a girlfriend!' because I haven't. I mean she isn't. You know what people are like. They start being embarrassing and saying stupid things – like Mum. If Tina rings me and Mum answers she stands at the bottom of the stairs holding the phone at arm's length and she shouts, so that everyone in the house (and Tina at the other end) can hear, 'Trevor! It's for you! It's Mrs Trevor . . .'

Pathetic, isn't it? That's Mum's sense of humour for you. Of course I do like Tina. She's smart and funny and so organized, which is very useful since I'm about as organized as the inside of a Christmas pudding. She's nice-looking too – but she's my friend, not my girlfriend. So hopefully you've got that straight.

Anyhow, Tina and I were in the field at the top of my road walking our dogs. Tina's dog is a giant St Bernard, with an enormous slobbery tongue. He doesn't lick you – it's more like being slapped about the face with a wet dishcloth. He's called Mouse. That was one of Tina's ideas, too.

Her dad thought she was bonkers. 'You can't call a dog that size Mouse. It's ridiculous!' Tina just smiled. That was the whole point. Tina thinks that most things are a bit ridiculous, and I guess she's right, sometimes.

My dog's TOTALLY ridiculous. We call her Streaker because she can run like the wind. Actually she runs more like a jet-propelled hurricane. When she's up to full speed she looks like one of those cartoon dogs, with her legs just a blur of frantic activity, and her ears flapping back in the slipstream. I sometimes think she's not actually a real dog at all and must have been built in a Ferrari factory. She could probably win a Grand Prix motor race if they let her take part. She'd have to wear a helmet though; a helmet with special holes for her ears. And they'd have to refuel her with dog food instead of petrol.

We used to have terrible trouble with Streaker. She didn't understand what her name was. She didn't know what was meant by 'Sit!' or 'Stay!' or 'Come back!' She'd just run and run and run. It was hopeless taking her for walks. For a start she didn't know what walking was. She could do

Run, Gallop, Full Charge Ahead, Fast Forward, Fast Reverse, Fast Sideways, Leaping Like Mad, Diving Like Mad, and generally being Madder than Mad – but walking? Oh no. If I let her off the lead I wouldn't get her back for hours. She drove the whole family bonkers.

Then Tina decided we would have to train her properly. (This was all because of a crazy bet we had with the local gorilla, Charlie Smugg. More on that later.) We tried all sorts of things, mostly to do with food and bribery, but none of them worked. Then, I thought that maybe we could exercise Streaker indoors instead of having to take her outside and losing her. We used my mum's exercise bike to build a dog-walking machine.

It sort of worked and sort of didn't. What I mean is, we made the machine, got it working, I grabbed Streaker, shouted 'Walkies!' and popped her on the running platform. Unfortunately the platform was revolving so fast it catapulted

Streaker backwards, right across the room and into the kitchen, where she got her bum jammed inside the washing machine. We had to get the fire brigade to come and rescue her.

The extraordinary thing was that after that dreadful experience, whenever I said 'Walkies!' to Streaker she came straight to my side and sat down very firmly, just in case I was planning to put her backside into the washer again. Perhaps she didn't fancy a quick wash and spin-dry. So now I have the only dog in the world that responds to the command 'Walkies!' by coming back to me and sitting down. She still doesn't know what 'Sit!' or 'Stay!' means, but at least she doesn't give us terrible trouble any longer. Nowadays she's only dreadful.

So – Tina and I were up at the field walking the dogs. It had been raining so it was a bit wet and muddy. Mouse was doing his usual thing of being very obedient and padding along quietly next to Tina, and Streaker was doing her usual thing of hurtling through the grass like an asteroid on four legs, crashing into anything and anyone she happened to come across. Sometimes there are other dog-walkers up at the field and when I let Streaker off the lead you can tell where she is because of all the shouts. 'Oh!', 'Ow!', 'Gerroff!' Every so often someone suddenly vanishes from sight altogether. That's because Streaker has just crashed into them and knocked them flying.

Tina was telling me about a programme she'd seen on television. 'This farmer was showing how good his dog was at herding sheep. The dog raced everywhere, keeping the sheep together in a tight herd. She drove all the sheep – a hundred of them – into a pen, just her and the farmer. A hundred sheep! Really clever.'

I nodded. 'Yeah, I've seen stuff like that, too.'

Tina grinned. 'And I thought: Streaker could do that.'

I stopped dead in my tracks and just gawped at her. 'Streaker? Herd sheep? You're crazy!' I stared across the field and watched as poor Mrs Potter suddenly gave a startled yell and went over like a skittle in a bowling alley. I sighed deeply. 'Streaker couldn't herd a leg of lamb,' I muttered.

'I bet she could,' Tina went on. 'We taught her how to come back, didn't we?'

'Oh sure we did. Just shout "Walkies!" and she comes back. That's clever, that is.'

Tina punched my arm. 'You're such a pessimist, Trev. Why don't we try? Streaker would be so good at it. The farmer on the programme said that all you needed was a dog that was intelligent . . .'

'Big problem there, then,' I moaned.

'. . . obedient . . .'

'Even bigger problem.'

'. . . and very fast.'

'That's about the only bit Streaker *can* do.'

'You give up so easily. We haven't even started.'

'Tina, we're not going to start. What's the point? Why teach Streaker how to herd sheep? Can you see any sheep around here for her to herd? No. There's lots of grass, several

abandoned shopping trolleys . . . hey, good idea, we could teach her to herd shopping trolleys!'

'Trev . . .'

'She could herd trolleys and drive them down the high street and back to the supermarket. That would be really useful.'

'Trevor! You're more out of control than your daft dog.'

'Aha! So you admit she's daft? That means she's not intelligent enough to be a sheepdog then.'

Tina sighed and we walked on in silence for a bit. Eventually she decided to tell me the real reason for her mad suggestion. 'It's just that there's a dog show coming up and I thought it would be fun to enter – you know, both of us.'

'We're not dogs,' I pointed out.

'You know what I mean. It's a big show and there are lots of different competitions – herding, best-looking, most obedient, agility – something for everyone.'

'Everyone except Streaker.'

'You are such a grumblepot.'

'No, I'm not. I know my dog's limitations. She can't do any of those things.'

'OK, suit yourself, but Mouse and I are still going to take part.'

'Yeah? Mouse is going to be the fattest, slowest

sheepdog in the show, is he?'

'No. I shall enter him for best-groomed dog.'

'Best groomed! He's a mess! He's all wet fur and droolly jaws and slobbery tongue. He looks like an exploding laundry.'

'He's only a mess at the moment, Trevor, that's all. By the time I'm finished with him he will look the business. I've got it all sorted and if you don't want to take part I'll do it on my own.

I'm going home now. There's no point in stomping round a field with a grobbling grumblepot.'

'No such word as *grobbling*,' I said.

'No such thing as an exploding laundry,' she snapped back, and off she went. Halfway across the field she shouted back at me, 'The trouble with you, Trevor, is that you have no imagination.'

That's what *she* thinks. In fact I have too much imagination. I know when it's just not worth attempting something that is sure to end in failure.

2 An Angel Appears

I carried on wandering aimlessly round the field
while Streaker continued her game of tenpin
bowling with the dog-walkers. It had started
drizzling but I was in a world of my own, staring
at the ground and trying to imagine Streaker
herding shopping trolleys stuffed with sheep.

'Hey! Watch where you're going!'

I looked up and – BAM!!

Right between the eyes. A vision, like an
angel. A girl so beautiful I couldn't take my eyes
off her face.

'You nearly walked straight into me,' she said.
I just stood there, staring at her, struck dumb.
'Hello? Anyone in? You almost knocked me over.'

'Sorry.'

'You looked as if you were in another world.'
She smiled and the sun came out. I don't mean
the real sun; it was still drizzling. It's just an
expression for the look on her face. I was wondering who this dazzling creature was, and where she
had come from. She had a crash-tested dog on a
lead. You know what I mean – one of those dogs
that look as if they've just run into a brick wall at
full speed and their face is all crumpled up.

'This is Roxy,' smiled the girl. 'She's a
pedigree.'

'I've not seen you up here before,' I began. In
the distance I could see Streaker hurtling
towards us like a bouncing bomb.

'I haven't been up here before,' the girl
answered. 'I've only recently moved here. So
what were you so deep in thought about?'

'I think you ought to move,' I said, my eyes on
Streaker.

She gave me an odd look. 'I *have* just moved.
We only got into the new house last month.'

'No, I mean now, this second, you ought to move . . .'

Streaker was rapidly getting closer and closer and bigger and bigger. Bounce, bounce, bounce . . .

'You're so weird,' laughed the girl. 'What do you . . . URRRFFF!!!'

Streaker cannoned straight into her back. She

was thrown off her feet and flung forwards. I reached out to stop her but her flying weight, with Streaker still attached, knocked me backwards and we all fell into the mud, with me underneath and the girl on top. Streaker happily jumped up and down on us a few times and then raced off to find some new victims.

The girl struggled to her feet.

'Look at me! Look at the mess I'm in! Look at – oh no! My jeans. They're all muddy!'

'Jeans are supposed to get muddy.' After all, I was in even more of a mess.

The girl gave me a scathing, scorching glance. 'Not *designer* jeans,' she hissed. 'These are Armani. My dad will be furious.' She bent down and twisted round to brush mud off her jeans. That was when I noticed her back. It was covered with doggy footprints that said 'Streaker was here – and here and here and here and HERE!!'

'I think you should . . .' I began and then thought better of it.

'What?' she snapped.

'Sorry,' I mumbled. 'Streaker gets a bit too friendly sometimes.'

'You mean that was *your* dog?!'

'It's nothing personal,' I said. 'She does it to everyone, including me.'

'You should train her.'

'She is trained. That's the best we could do. You should have seen her before. Anyhow, I did tell you to move.'

'That's not good enough. You're only making excuses.'

'You sound like one of my teachers,' I muttered.

'Really? Are you as badly behaved as your dog then?' She examined her jeans yet again.

I sighed. For goodness' sake, they were only jeans!

'And look at my trainers – they're filthy! My dad's going to be so angry. You'll be hearing more about this. Do you know who he is?'

I shook my head and pointed out that I didn't even know who she was.

'Melinda,' she scowled. 'Melinda Boffington-Orr. And my dad is . . .'

'. . . Mr Boffington-Orr?' I suggested brightly.

'Exactly. And you are?'

'Trevor – but you can call me Trevor.'

Melinda screwed up her nose. 'What's that supposed to mean?'

'Nothing. It's a joke.'

'Funny kind of joke.'

I nodded. 'Yep. That's the best kind, I think – funny ones.'

'Yours wasn't. Now get out of my way. I'm going home.'

And off she went, squelch, squelch, squelch,

Melinda Boffington-Orr, the girl of my dreams. I stood in the drizzle and watched. I still had no idea who Mr Boffington-Orr was, but I had a feeling I was going to find out pretty soon.

3 The Boffington-Orrs

Dad stood at the bottom of the stairs, peering into the hall mirror and fiddling with his shirt. 'Get a move on, Trevor!'

'Do I really have to wear a tie?'

'Yes! We're going to the Golf Club Dinner Dance, and you're not allowed in without a tie.'

I hate wearing a tie. They're just so, so – poxy. I always feel like an idiot when I've got one on. (I feel like an idiot most of the time anyway, but now I was an idiot with a tie – yuk.) And I hate golf too, and the clubhouse.

Dad plays golf as often as he can. He loves it, but I can't see the point. You get a very small ball and a very long stick. You hit the ball as far as you can. Then you walk after it, and when you find it (which might take some time, depending on where it landed) you hit it again. Then you walk after it, and when you see it you hit it again. Then you walk after it, and when you see it you . . . and so on, and so on. Every so often the ball might go down a hole. Then you get excited. And after you've got excited what do you do next? You hit the ball again and then you walk after it . . .

Dad likes clay-pigeon shooting, too. That's the one where you have a shotgun. You shout 'Pull!' and a disc flies up in the air (that's the 'pigeon') and you shoot it down. Now, I reckon Dad ought to play *clay golf*, which is a game I've invented for golfers and shooters. The golfer sends his ball whizzing through the air and the shooter has to shoot it down. Brilliant, eh?! It would make golf *so* much more interesting.

Anyhow, Dad seems to like the pointlessness of golf and he's got all these chums up at the club. Every so often they get together for a dinner and sometimes they bring their families along. Aren't we lucky? As you can imagine, I was so looking forward to it.

Mum came out of the bedroom and wandered past my door. Wow! She was wearing a dress! I've hardly ever seen Mum in a dress. She spends most of her time in a tracksuit or running gear. She does weight training and aerobics and stuff. (Hey, listen, Tina told me this joke, but it's a bit rude, so don't tell your mum or dad, OK? What do you call PE exercises in the nude? Bareobics. Ha ha!)

The golf club is pretty posh. It's not just for golfers – there's a swimming pool there and a gymnasium that Mum goes to. You have to pay to be a member and not only that, you have to be examined by a committee to see if you're suitable for membership. If you're badly behaved you can get thrown out. (Would you believe not wearing a tie counts as bad behaviour!)

So Mum was all poshed up and Dad was all poshed up and I was forced into a tie and was trying hard not to look too poshed up. That was how we arrived at the clubhouse, and the first person I saw was – Melinda. Melinda Boffington-Orr. My heart changed gear several times until it was in overdrive. I didn't care that she was scowling at me. She still looked stunning.

'Oh, it's you,' she said. 'What are you doing here?'

'My dad's a member.'

'Really? The committee obviously didn't know anything about you then.'

This conversation was going so well! I thought that maybe Melinda would have recovered from her sprawl in the mud, but no, she was still seething. I had to make things up to her somehow.

'I did say I was sorry and I did try to warn

you. I couldn't do much more, could I?'

Before she could answer a large man came wandering across. He was not only tall, he was overloaded. (OK – he was fat.) He looked very smart in a dark suit, but he had a big belly and massive shoulders. He had a chin like a brick and his lower lip stuck out further than his top lip, reminding me very strongly of Roxy. He gave me a cheerful smile. He had a gold tooth that glistened.

'Hello, Melinda. Making a new friend?'

'Not exactly, Daddy. This is Trevor. Trevor from the field, you remember? Trevor with the dog. Trevor the mud expert.'

Mr Boffington-Orr looked down at me from his great height. The smile had become a dark scowl. (So that's where Melinda got it from!) 'Ah, so you're the lad that ruined my daughter's jeans? Do you know how much those cost me? Have you any idea? Do I look as if I'm made of money?'

I was thinking, well, yes, you do look as if

you're made of money. You've got a gold tooth for starters. You've obviously got a lot more money than my parents. Heaps more.

I could see Dad in the distance, laughing with an attractive woman on the far side of the room. She took his arm, pulling him towards the dance floor. I groaned inwardly and hoped he wasn't going to dance. Dad's a hopeless dancer. Then I saw Mum coming towards us. My heart began to thump. I could feel a Moment of Doom approaching fast.

'Your dog is a liability,' continued Mr B-O. (You don't mind me calling him that, do you? No, I didn't think you would.) 'She should be trained properly. Dogs like that shouldn't be allowed on the streets.'

Mum arrived, beaming. 'Mr Boffington-Orr, what a delight! Trevor, this is . . .'

'I know,' I said miserably.

'This your son?' growled B-O. 'He ruined my daughter's clothes. Him and his dog.'

'What?'

There it was, the

MOMENT OF DOOM.

Boffington-Orr gave a more than full description of events. I say it was more than full

25

because B-O himself had not actually been there and now he was exaggerating rather a lot. Melinda added her scathing comments from time to time, just to make sure I was totally scuppered. Not that it mattered because now B-O was staring across the room. He kept sticking one finger between his neck and his collar and making strange thrusting movements with his big chin, so that it jutted out even further.

Dad was on the dance floor, swinging his arms and legs like a deranged baboon. (It's the only

way he knows how to dance.) The attractive woman was laughing and encouraging him. He took hold of her hand and they began to twirl round. Mum and I both sighed at the same time.

'If only he could see what he looks like,' she said quietly.

'Do you know that man?' growled Boffington-Orr.

'Of course. He's my husband.'

'Your husband! I might have known.'

Boffington-Orr strode towards the whirling couple, but it was too late. All of a sudden the dancers made one fast move too many. They got completely entangled, tripped each other up and crashed to the floor in a giggling, squirming heap. B-O only got there in time to haul the woman to her feet. Dad climbed to his knees, still chuckling.

'What do you think you're doing?' demanded B-O.

'Dancing,' laughed Dad.

'That wasn't dancing. That was mauling.'

The woman put a hand on B-O's shoulder. 'Darling, we were just having fun.'

Darling! Uh-oh. That must be Mrs B-O!!

'Your behaviour was disgusting,' snapped Boffington-Orr, addressing my father. 'And that is just what I have come to expect from your family. You're a bunch of yobs.'

'Just a moment . . .' began Dad, but B-O wouldn't let him finish.

'You come here and make an exhibition of yourself, mauling my wife. No wonder your son doesn't know how to behave, pushing my daughter in the mud, and that dog of yours ought to be put down.'

It felt as if a deep, deep hole had just opened right beneath my feet. I could feel myself falling. 'Dad?' I croaked.

Even my dad was shocked. He took a step back from B-O. 'Just hold on there, I don't think you should make comments like that about our dog. Streaker might be a little wild at times but . . .'

'A little wild? She ruined Melinda's clothes. She might have bitten her.'

'Streaker has never bitten anyone!' I shouted.

'Keep quiet, Trevor,' snapped Dad. He turned to Melinda's father. 'I'm sorry your daughter's clothes were damaged. If you send them to our house we shall see what we can do to clean them. As for Streaker, I think you should keep your comments about her to yourself.'

Mr Boffington-Orr drew himself to his full height – which was pretty impressive. Now his voice took on an ultra-cold quality – so cold it felt as if large icebergs were tumbling from his mouth and crushing everyone as he spoke.

'You consider your position carefully. Evidently you have no idea who I am. I am the new chairman of the golf-club committee. I also happen to be the new police superintendent for this town. Get that dog trained, or you'll be hearing from me again, and you won't like that, I can promise you.'

'Are you threatening me?' Dad answered, just as coldly.

'Yes. In fact, I will tell you what's going to happen. There's a dog show coming up soon and the Police Federation is sponsoring it. Your dog can take part.'

'Don't be ridiculous,' Dad laughed. 'You can't possibly be serious.'

'Oh, I am,' the superintendent smiled. 'Think of it as a Community Service Order for your dog. I shall expect to see your mutt there. My sergeant down at the station is entering his three Alsatians. I shall expect your dog to beat at least one of them. If she doesn't you can kiss goodbye to your membership of this golf club. And it will be very bad news for your dog, too. I'll not have dangerous dogs in my town.'

'Dangerous?' exploded Dad.

'Dangerous,' repeated B-O, in a threateningly quiet voice.

There was a long silence. You don't mess with

a police superintendent, especially when they're also chairman of the golf club. That's what Dad was thinking. I could tell.

B-O gave a grim smile, draped one arm round Melinda, imprisoned his wife with the other, turned away and they walked off. You could almost hear them sniggering to each other.

4 Best-Groomed Dog?

Dad's been going about the place looking as if war has been declared and he's just discovered enemy submarines in his bath. He might get thrown out of the golf club! The shame of it! The disgrace! Then he'd get all furious and start shouting about that bullying, arrogant Boffington-Orr. And of course I'd catch it because of Streaker.

'She'll have to be trained properly,' Dad kept snapping. 'Either that or we shall have to find a new home for her. We could put her into a dogs' home.'

This wasn't anything new to me. Every time Streaker did something really awful Dad suggested putting her into a home. But this was Trouble – Big Time!! It came with capital letters and exclamation marks and frowns added. Dad felt he was personally under attack and was seriously considering re-homing Streaker.

I couldn't think what to do. There was only one person I could talk to – Tina. I took Streaker up to the field, sat on a log and waited. Tina was bound to show up with Mouse sooner or later, and she did. She sat down next to me, and Mouse sat down next to her. It would have been nice if Streaker had come and sat beside me and made a full set, but she was trying to be a squirrel. She was leaping up the trunk of a tree, trying to climb it and then wondering why she kept falling backwards and landing on her bum in the bushes.

I was really pleased to see Tina, but she seemed a bit cold towards me.

'What are you doing here?' she asked.

'Walking the dog. If you remember I always walk the dog here.'

'Oh. You still walk her then.'

'What's that supposed to mean?'

'I've come up here to train Mouse for the dog show,' Tina said coolly.

'Why are you still on about that?'

Tina shuffled her feet and when I looked at her face I was surprised to see she'd gone red.

'Because I thought it would be fun to train our two dogs together and because . . . because I thought we were friends.'

'We are friends. We've been friends for ages.'

'Trevor. Try not to be stupid. I mean – *friends*.'

'Oh,' I said, still completely in the dark. '*Friends*.' Inside I was thinking: Help! What's she on about now?

Tina shuffled her feet a bit more. The grass below was getting a really tough deal from Tina's feet. 'I saw you with that girl,' she muttered.

'What girl?'

'The one with the long hair – the long, blonde hair, and the boxer dog.'

'That was Melinda Boffington-Orr,' I said. 'She's beautiful.' If looks could kill I'd be dead. Tina's eyes were turning into flame-throwers and I was shrivelling beneath their gaze. 'What? What did I say?'

Tina took a deep breath. 'It doesn't matter, Trev. It's not what you say, it's what you think.'

'But I wasn't thinking anything!'

'Well maybe that's the problem, Trev. Maybe you should start thinking.'

I frowned. 'What are we talking about?' I asked eventually. 'I've sort of completely lost the plot.'

'Doesn't matter,' said Tina. 'So, what's been going on with Melinda then?'

Ah! Now I could tell Tina the whole story, so I did. She laughed a lot at the bit when Melinda fell in the mud – I'm not sure why. She laughed again when Dad fell over with Mrs B-O. She said that Dad and I were like peas in a pod.

(How could she say that!) Then I got to the bit about Mr Boffington-Orr being the Most Important Person In The Universe.

'I hate people like that,' Tina declared.

'He's too big for his boots. Come to think of it, he's just too big. You should see his chin, it's like the shovel on a JCB.'

Tina was quiet for several minutes. Mouse curled up at her feet. (Actually curled isn't the right word because St Bernards can't do curling. They can only do throwing-themselves-on-the-floor-in-a-big-messy-lump.) Even so I found myself wishing that Streaker was more like Mouse. I stared across the field, wondering where she was now. She'd stopped doing squirrel impressions long ago. A lady walking round the far edge of the field suddenly vanished with a startled cry. Ah, that'd be Streaker. I sighed.

'So your dog's in trouble again,' Tina observed. 'And she's got to take part in the dog show after all.'

'Yep.'

'If she gets reported to the police or anything things could get quite nasty for her.'

I nodded. 'Suppose so.'

A little smile crept across Tina's face. 'So it would be a really, REALLY good idea if Streaker did some more training. It could save her life.'

I should have seen it coming, shouldn't I? I expect you could see what Tina was working towards all the time. The trouble is, I couldn't. She always manages to catch me out and before I know it, BAM! She's hit me with the unanswerable argument. She looked straight at me, victory in her eyes.

'Wouldn't it?' she repeated. 'Wouldn't it be a good idea?'

'All right,' I groaned. 'Maybe it would be sensible, but what kind of training should she do?'

Tina suddenly perked up. Now she was full of smiles and encouragement. 'Why don't you bring Streaker over to my house and we can work on both the dogs together.'

'OK, what are you doing with Mouse?'

'I told you, he's entered for best-groomed dog.'

'Tina! How am I supposed to groom Streaker? She's not a pedigree. She's just an ordinary mutt.'

'The trouble is, you're looking at Streaker the wrong way. You were telling me earlier that Melinda B-O is a bit snooty, but you also said she was beautiful. So she has a beautiful outside, but an ugly inside. Appearances are deceptive. Maybe some things can look ugly from the outside but be beautiful on the inside.'

'So when the judges at the dog show come along and start examining Streaker, what do I do – turn her inside out? Get all her guts out and spread them around and say: "Look! Isn't it pretty! Sorry about the blood everywhere, but she has such pretty kidneys!"'

Tina stopped dead, hands on hips. 'Trevor, you know perfectly well that's not what I meant.'

'No, but what you said was funny, that's all.'

'The thing is, if people can be like that then animals can be too, I'm sure. We can groom Streaker and prettify her. Come on, up to the bathroom. Mum's next door helping the neighbour make a birthday cake. His wife will be ninety tomorrow so it has to be a special cake apparently, very soft, easy to eat, because she hasn't got any teeth left.'

We headed upstairs with the two dogs. Streaker

got very excited when she saw water running into the tub. Streaker doesn't often get bathed in our house. I had a sneaking suspicion that she would not get bathed very often in Tina's house after this either, but I didn't tell her. Why spoil the fun?

'Give me a hand with Mouse. He can't get in on his own.'

Boy oh boy! That dog weighed a ton. No, I tell a lie – ten tons. I practically broke my back lifting him. Mouse sat down and a big wave of water slopped over the top. Tina got some shampoo – 'Hair Care for Big Dogs, with Fig Oil and Dandelion Milk for Added Bounce and Extra Shine. Also contains Calcium Supplement for Strong Bones'. I pointed out that hair doesn't have bones in it.

'I expect the calcium soaks in somehow and gets to the bones that way,' Tina said.

'I expect it's a rip-off,' I said.

'Rub it in all over,' muttered Tina, and we got to work, lathering up Mouse.

Q. What do dogs do when they get wet?

A. They give themselves a good shake.

And the bigger the dog is the wetter it gets, and the bigger and wetter they are the more they have to shake. And the more they shake the further all the water gets flung. Bathing Mouse was like sitting next to the Niagara Falls. Wet.

As we worked up the shampoo Mouse seemed to get even larger. I think Tina might have squirted on a bit too much. He was beginning to look like a major accident in a soap factory.

'The shampoo has to soak in for ten minutes,' Tina explained, just as Mouse gave himself another grand shake and coated the walls (and us) with big flecks of shampoo.

'Oh good,' I said, flicking shampoo from the end of my nose. 'My hair will be so nice and shiny by then. And so will my skin and my clothes and the bathroom walls and the ceiling and –'

'Shut up, misery guts,' interrupted Tina. 'We'll do Streaker while we're waiting. There's room in

the tub for both dogs.'

Tina was right about the amount of room in the bath. However, she hadn't allowed for the fact that Streaker moves about quite a lot. In fact it is probably what Streaker does best of all – move about. She's a real expert, and she can do it without stopping for hours. Once Tina had squirted Streaker with a bit of shampoo it was impossible to get hold of her at all. She just kept slipping out of our hands. It was like trying to find a giant bar of soap in the water. Every time we grabbed her she just went – bloooop! – and shot out the other end.

'I'll get Mouse cleaned off. Then it will be

easier,' Tina sighed. She got the shower head
and started to wash down Mouse. That was all
right until Streaker grabbed hold of the snaking
shower hose and tore it from Tina's grasp. Water
spurted everywhere.

Tina shouted at Streaker and tried to grab it
back, but that just made Streaker think it was all
a game. We weren't sitting next to Niagara Falls
any longer – we were actually in it. Streaker
barked and growled and crouched and jumped.
Tina grasped the hose and pulled and a tug of

war began which could only have one possible result – which quickly happened. Tina fell into the bath.

So there's Mouse in the bath all wet and bedraggled, and Streaker in the bath, still with the shower head in her mouth, busily making sure that there wasn't anything dry anywhere within ten miles, and Tina in the bath struggling to clamber out but not being able to because the sides were so slippery with soap and anyhow the dogs kept knocking her over, and me standing there, watching and laughing and laughing and getting totally soaked . . .

. . . and in walks Tina's mum.

So that was the end of Streaker's grooming session. I've been banned from Tina's house for two weeks. The dog show comes up in two weeks' time and I don't know what to do. Help!

5 The Return of Charlie Smugg

Tina's mum only went and told my dad, didn't she? She rang him up to complain, and while Dad was talking to Mrs Angry on the phone the postman came to the door with a parcel. Do you know what it was? Melinda Boffington-Orr's muddy Armani jeans and top. There was a note inside.

Dear Mr Larkey,
If you are unable to get these clothes properly cleaned then you will have to replace them or send a cheque for their full value, £124.98.
Your dog should be fully trained, kept on a lead and muzzled. If I hear of any further misdemeanours regarding her I shall issue an order for her to be

destroyed. Your membership of the golf club is also in
serious doubt.

  Yours sincerely,

Boris Boffington-Orr

Boris Boffington-Orr
Chief Superintendent,
Chairman of Swankyman Golf Club,
Ex-7th Eltham Scout Troupe,
Black Belt Tae Kwon Do,
Blue Peter Badge-Holder (Twice).

Was my dad a happy man by the time he had finished the phone call and read the note? Of course he wasn't. Did he do his extraordinarily accurate impression of

The End Of The World As We Know It, featuring full volcanic eruptions, several hurricanes and multiple earthquakes complete with collapsing buildings? Of course he did. And you can guess who caught the worst of it. That's right. Me. Dad's final words were something like 'Get that dog trained or she'll have to go.'

I took Streaker to the field. 'It's not my fault,' I told her as we walked up the road. She looked at me with her shining eyes and wagged her tail cheerfully. 'It's not exactly your fault, either,' I told her. 'After all, you're a dog.'

Streaker gave a little jump and a single bark. An elderly lady stopped with her wheeled shopping bag and smiled.

'That's a lovely dog,' she said and before I could stop her she was patting Streaker on the head.

Oh dear. That was a mistake.

Streaker doesn't normally get pats on the head because she is far too over-excited for anyone to get that close to her, but somehow this little old

lady managed it. Streaker was so gobsmacked she
leaped into the air – just like that – as if she had
a pogo stick attached to each leg. Ker-poinnggg!

The 'up' bit of the jump was fine. The trouble
is that once something has jumped up it has to
come down somewhere. Streaker came down on
the lady's shoulders and she promptly collapsed in
a heap on her shopping
bag, which set off
down the hill at high
speed.

Streaker thought this
was terrific. A free
ride! She got to her
feet, standing on the old
lady's shoulders and
began to bark madly at
everything and every-
one. The old lady was
screaming her head off,
waving and kicking and

making a dreadful racket. Everyone was staring. Well they would, wouldn't they? It's not often you see a barking, screaming shopping bag on wheels travelling at full speed, waving arms and legs at you.

And then, just before something truly awful could happen, the bag split open and came to a grinding halt. The shopping went every which way and so did the old lady. Streaker jumped off and ran back to me with a big grin on her face, while the old lady struggled to her feet and shouted after us.

'I'll tell the police about this! Where do you come from? What's your name? Where do you live?'

'Venus!' I yelled back and hurried off. Phew. Lucky escape.

As if the morning was not already bad enough, when I got to the field, who was there? Charlie Smugg and his three Alsatians.

Let me introduce Charlie Smugg. He's the

local gorilla. No, that's not fair – gorillas are quiet, peaceful, well-behaved animals that only become dangerous when they are well and truly cornered. Charlie Smugg, however, is dangerous at all times, and he's an oaf. He's fourteen and enormous – built like a tank. Almost everything about Charlie is big. He only has one small bit in his body – and that's his brain.

Tina and I got into serious trouble with Charlie last year when he bet us we couldn't train Streaker to do anything. There's an old horse trough in the corner of the field, full of gunky muck. Charlie said if we lost the bet we would both have to get in the trough and wash our hair. Talk about yuck! And of course if he lost the bet then he had to get in. Well, that was when Tina and I made the dog-walking machine and Streaker got trained to come back.

So Charlie lost the bet and should have got in the trough, but surprise, surprise he wouldn't, and we certainly couldn't make him. But he was still angry with us. Matters were not helped by the fact that his dad was the sergeant at the police station where Mr B-O was now top dog. All the Smuggs like to throw their weight around, and they've got a lot of weight to throw, too.

The Smuggs have got three Alsatians and they are lethal. Why should anyone want three of the beasts? They're really scary dogs, all bark and bite. They'd love to eat Streaker but fortunately she's much too fast for them, and a lot cleverer.

So at the field there was Charlie with his three

dogs and a scrambler bike. It sounded as if there was a very large, angry wasp on the loose. Neeeyaaaaarrrrrr!! And the bike went whizzing and bouncing across the field, with the dogs in pursuit. I must say it seemed a pretty good way to exercise them.

Charlie soon spotted me and I could see the

bike coming straight over. He skidded to a halt, sending a flurry of mud and stones over my shoes, sat back and grinned. 'Well well, if it ain't Clever Trevor. Whadda you think of my bike?'

'It's all right.'

'SIT!' Charlie suddenly roared as the three Alsatians caught up with him. They sat instantly, in a row, slavering and showing their enormous fangs.

'Dad's got a bike, too,' boasted Charlie. 'He's gonna do a display at the dog show.'

'Your dad's not a dog,' I said, although secretly I was thinking of Sergeant Smugg as a chihuahua.

'Oh ha ha,' sneered Charlie. 'The superin- tendent has asked my dad to put a display team together and

I'm gonna be in it. Dad's gonna ride the bike, with eight people standing on his shoulders.'

'That will help solve the traffic problem,' I muttered.

'Yeah, and I'm gonna put the dogs in the show – agility. I'm gonna win an' all.'

'No chance,' I crowed. 'Streaker's going to win that.'

Oh bums! Why did I have to say that!

I knew I shouldn't have said it even as the words came out of my mouth, but it was too late. Charlie pounced.

'Ha! Streaker? Beat my dogs? Don't be stupid.'

'Streaker could beat your dogs any day. She's doing the agility test, too.'

Charlie's eyes narrowed. 'Do you wanna make that a bet? Same as before?'

OK, now listen to me. You know I'm not stupid. I'm not, am I? Certainly not as stupid as Charlie Smugg. So what happens? Do I show how clever I am and say: 'No Charlie, I do not want to make a bet with you. That would be such a silly, foolish thing to do considering how things turned out last time.' Do I say that? No. What do I say?

'Sure, I bet you.'

DOH! (As someone famous says.)

So that is how I ended up getting myself into even deeper trouble. Now I had a bet with Charlie and it's the animal trough for me if Streaker doesn't beat the Smuggs' Alsatians. Just to finish my day totally I discovered something else about Charlie.

He started up his bike and was revving the engine to show off. I wanted to get back at him somehow because I was feeling so low, so I asked him how Sharon was. (Tina and I once caught Charlie holding hands with Sharon Blenkinsop – he was so embarrassed! Talk about a face like a beetroot!)

Now he just grinned at me. 'Dumped her ages ago,' he said. 'Going out with someone else now. She's totally cute AND she's my dad's boss's daughter. Her name's Melinda. Oh yeah, something else – that bet we just made. Don't forget that includes *your* girlfriend! See ya, dumbhead!'

The bike snarled and spat more mud and stones over me and off it went, with the Alsatians lolloping after it.

The clouds came down, heavy black clouds. I tramped home feeling about as miserable as it was possible to feel. It seemed to me that the entire world was against me. Even Streaker had her tail between her legs.

6 What Kind of Noise Does a Squirrel Make?

'You said *what*?!'

There. I knew Tina would be impressed.

'You are such an idiot!'

OK, maybe she wasn't impressed.

'I cannot believe you would do something so incredibly, pathetically stupid.'

Definitely not impressed.

'You are a total mashed potato.'

Mashed potato? That was a new one on me. 'Mashed potato?' I repeated back to her.

'As in brain like a . . . got it?'

I nodded dumbly. Tina sat on the edge of my bed, staring into her lap and frowning. She shook her head. 'You've landed us both in it now. If you'd stayed quiet we could have kept the whole thing secret and then sprung it as a surprise. Now Charlie will be on the lookout, and so will his dad.'

Of course. Sergeant Smugg. I'd forgotten about him for a moment. He would be watching out for any opportunity to make Streaker's life difficult, just so that his own dogs had a better chance of winning.

'What are we going to do?' I moaned.

There was a long silence before Tina spoke. She got up, walked around the room, gazed out of the window, walked around again, picked at the wallpaper and finally sat down once more.

'OK, let's sort out this mess. We have to get Streaker trained. That will get Boffy-Offywotsit off Streaker's back, not to mention your mum and dad. Then we have to beat the Smuggs' Alsatians in the agility test at the dog show.'

I nodded glumly. 'And don't forget about Melinda,' I added.

'Melinda?'

'I've got to put things right with her.'

'Why's that?' Tina was looking at me search-
ingly. Faint alarm bells were starting to ring
somewhere in my mind.

'Well, we got off to a bad start and I'd really
like it if we could be friends.'

'Why's that?'

I wished Tina didn't keep asking 'Why's that?'
all the time!

'Because she's . . . um . . .' I wanted to say
that Melinda was beautiful and gorgeous and
made my heart leap every time I saw her but I
couldn't really tell Tina that. 'She's . . . nice.' I
finished lamely.

'Oh good. I'm glad,' Tina answered frostily.
'I'm so glad she's . . . *nice*.' Tina made the word
'nice' sound as if she'd just got it out of the deep
freeze and dropped it down the back of my neck.

'Actually Trevor, I don't know if you have real-
ized but we have a small crisis to deal with

concerning Streaker. Forget Melinda and think about your dog for a moment or two. I think we should train Streaker at the old football ground.'

'But it's a shambles! Nobody goes there. It's full of old tyres and stuff.'

'Exactly. It will be ideal. If nobody's there we won't be spotted and we can use all the junk lying around to build our own agility course.'

The more I thought about it the better it seemed. Tina was right. The old football ground would be ideal. Nobody would ever know what we were up to and we could get on with the training in peace and quiet.

We went down there at once. It's a bit further away than the field, and I hadn't been there for a while, but it hadn't changed much. The local football team used to play there but that had been years earlier. It had been deserted for ages. Nobody seemed to know what to do with it and people who lived anywhere near just used it as a kind of unofficial dump. Where footballers had once rushed about shouting 'To me! To me!' at each other, there were now a dozen abandoned cars. Everywhere there was refuse – not the small rubbish you put in bins, but big rubbish, like old sheds people didn't want any longer, lumps of concrete, tyres, old fridges, spin dryers – not to mention the cars.

Streaker thought it was brilliant and went whizzing around happily, trying to sniff every-thing at once. Tina grabbed an old car tyre and dropped it by my feet.

'We need ten of these,' she said. 'We'll put them in a row, leaving a good gap between each one.'

'A slalom course!' I shouted.

'Exactly. Come on.'

It didn't take long to find the tyres. However, getting Streaker to weave her way in and out of them was another matter. She jumped on them. She ran across them. She ran between them. She sat on them, lay down on them, barked at

them and finally she widdled on them. Then she
ran off.

Tina gazed after the disappearing hound. 'I
didn't think she'd do it straight away, but I did
think she'd have a better go at it than that.'

'We're dead,' I groaned.

'Trevor! We've only just begun. You can't give
up straight away. In fact you can't give up at all.'

'All right.' I sighed. 'What other things do the

dogs have to do for the agility test?'

'Slalom, See-Saw, Tunnel, Hoop and Wall of Death.'

'What's the Wall of Death?'

'It's where they have to scramble up a really high wall and down the other side,' Tina explained. That perked me up a little.

'OK. We'll try that next.' I said. 'You know how Streaker likes to climb trees? She could be good at this.'

So while I went off to try and get Streaker back Tina began work on the Wall of Death. By the time I returned she'd unearthed a huge sheet of plywood and was trying to drag it across the ground. It was far too heavy.

'Hang on, I'll give you a hand.' We managed to lift it upright and rest it against the rusty cabin of an old van. The effort left us both panting and wiping the dirt from our hands. Tina grinned.

'We make a good team,' she said. 'Just you and me.'

'Yeah.'

'Can't imagine Melinda Toffee-Boffee-Offywotsit getting herself dirty like this.'

Do you ever feel as if you've suddenly been hit on the back of the head by an invisible boomerang? Well that's the kind of effect Tina's remark had on me. I stopped dead in my tracks, unable to think of a smart answer.

Tina smiled triumphantly. 'You're pretty strong,' she added, changing the subject. 'Muscles like iron. I bet your mum makes you eat loads of Brussels sprouts.'

Now she was making me blush!

'Come on. Let's see if Streaker does the business.'

I took Streaker to the wall and let her sniff it. She put her front paws against it and scrabbled a bit. 'That's it! Jump up! Good girl!' Streaker gave a half-hearted jump.

'You'll have to get her to run at it and then scramble up,' Tina pointed out.

All three of us ran at the wall, shouting and barking. (Tina and I were shouting; the dog was barking, in case you were wondering.) We crashed into the wall.

'That wasn't quite what we wanted you to do, Streaker,' I told her. 'Let's try that again.'

We hurled ourselves at the wall once more but Streaker just didn't seem to get the idea that she had to climb up it.

'I know what's wrong,' I said. 'When Streaker goes up trees she's going after squirrels, right? You get up on the roof of the van, hide behind the top of the wall and make squirrel noises, OK?'

'What sort of noises do squirrels make?'

'Don't know. Wheep wheep? Eee-eee-eeeek? Try one of those.'

Tina climbed on to the van roof and lay down behind the wall. I took Streaker a long way back so she had a good run-up. 'Are you ready?'

'Ready!' cried Tina.

'OK, go for it!'

An incredible din rose from the Wall of Death. It sounded like a whole bunch of balloons having their necks pinched while air was squeezed out of them. Streaker and I hurtled towards the wall.

'Eeeeeeeek!' screamed Tina.

And then, BANG! We reached the wall and Streaker just thundered up it at a billion miles an hour, straight into Tina's arms. Brilliant!

We were so excited. Streaker jumped up and down. Tina jumped up and down. Streaker threw herself from the roof and landed in my arms. We fell to the ground and she rolled off, leaping and barking, her eyes shining. I scrambled to my feet.

'My turn!' yelled Tina and she threw herself from the van roof too, knocking me straight back on to the ground. 'We did it!' she shouted.

'You make a pretty good squirrel,' I laughed, sitting up.

Tina leaned against me, panting. 'That was great. All we have to do now is the tunnel, see-saw and hoop.'

'And the slalom,' I added. We were quiet for a
bit, getting over the excitement. 'You were right
about this being a good place to come.'

'Yes. But I've got a question for you, Trev. Do
you think Melinda would make a good squirrel?'

Oh boy! Would she? I had no idea at all. But
it was an interesting thought.

7 The Knicker Nicker

Guess who the next person I saw was? Yep, that's right – Melinda. I knew it was her immediately even though she was some way ahead of me as I walked Streaker home. I quickened my steps so that I could catch her up and all the time I was thinking: so what do I say to her when I do catch up with her? And then I was walking next to her, a bit out of breath.

'Hi!'

'Oh, it's you. Mudboy.'

'Trevor.' I nodded and flashed my best smile at her.

'Your front teeth are crooked,' she said. 'My daddy says you should never trust anyone with crooked teeth.'

'I can't help it,' I mumbled. 'I didn't ask anyone for teeth like these. They just sort of arrived
in my mouth like this.'

And now I was thinking: this conversation is
stupid! I want to tell her how lovely she is and
here we are talking about crooked teeth!

I made a huge effort to try and change the
conversation. 'Your teeth are lovely,' I said.
'Nice, straight teeth. You're lucky. You got sent
straight teeth. I got sent wonky ones.'

Melinda flashed me an odd look. 'Are you
weird, or something? Do you always talk to
people like this? Daddy says you can't trust weird
people.'

I struggled not to be too weird and tried to
think of something interesting to say. I gazed at
her dog. 'What make of dog is that?'

'Make?' Melinda rolled her eyes scornfully.
'She's not a car, stupid. She's a boxer. I'm entering her in the dog show.'

'Really? How's the training going?'

Melinda gave a snort. She sounded a bit like a small pony – a very pretty, small pony. 'We don't have to do that sort of stuff. Roxy is already trained – unlike some dogs I could mention.'

'What are you entering her for?'

'Best in Show of course. That means she does everything. She's bound to win. Roxy's a pedigree. She cost Daddy hundreds. Do you know what her proper name is? Wisteria Wannabee Winstanley the Eighth.'

I gulped. That was a bit of a mouthful and certainly not the sort of name you would want to shout out in the middle of a field. No wonder they called her Roxy.

'Pedigree dogs always have a proper name,' Melinda went on. 'It's because they are so special, and expensive. You can call mongrels anything you like.'

'I know, we call Streaker all sorts! You should hear my dad sometimes. He calls her things like Bottomsniffer and Dopey-Deaf-Mutt.'

'That's not what I meant,' grumbled Melinda. 'Although I can easily imagine your father saying crude things like that.'

I had the impression that I wasn't getting much further with Melinda.

'My daddy says you can't trust a man who says rude words.'

'Right.' Long silence. But I had to ask eventually. The question was beginning to burn a hole in my tongue. 'Does your dad trust anyone?'

Melinda stopped, turned, faced me square on and gave me a dazzling smile, her neat white

teeth flashing in the sun. 'He doesn't trust you,' she said. 'Or your dog, or anyone in your family for that matter. Goodbye.'

And off she went, leaving me feeling as if she had just sucked every bone out of my body and left me in a heap of flabby skin on the pavement, slowly dribbling away over the kerb and into the gutter and down the drain. And she still looked beautiful!

Somehow I managed to drag myself home, although as you can imagine it was very difficult with no bones left.

The first thing I noticed when I reached the house was that Dad had crooked teeth. I asked Mum if having crooked teeth made you a crooked person. She almost fell off her exercise bike.

'Don't be daft. That's like saying that the more freckles you have the more stupid you are, or that if you've got small ears you must be deaf. You can't help what you're born with, Trevor. Teeth just sort of come out the way they are, and the only way to change them is to go to the dentist and have them rearranged. Anyhow, what's all this about teeth?'

So I told Mum about Melinda and what she had said and Mum began laughing all over again. 'The cheek of it! I bet that girl's teeth aren't naturally straight. I bet she's had work done on them. Probably cost a fortune.' She stopped pedalling and looked at me. 'You like Melinda, don't you?'

'It's not like that, Mum!'

'I don't suppose it is. I don't suppose she'll let

74

you anywhere near, not after shoving her in the mud.'

'That was Streaker. I don't see why I should keep getting the blame for that.'

'No, but you can understand why she's wary of you. Listen, if you want to make a good impression you should do something nice for her. Make her a card. Buy her a chocolate bar or pick some flowers for her. Something like that.'

Mum began pedalling again and I went off to do some thinking. Maybe Mum was right. I could try that. Make a good impression. Get Melinda something nice. Then she'd be really pleased and she'd like me.

Yep – it was an excellent idea. I grabbed some dosh from my money pile and headed down the high street. I stood outside the flower shop for ages but I couldn't make up my mind. Red roses? Those yellow things? Eventually I gave up on flowers. Maybe I could find something in one of the big department stores.

By this time I was beginning to think of jewellery. Obviously I wasn't going to get Melinda diamonds or pearls, but I thought I might be able to find a nice bracelet or little necklace. The accessory department was right next to Ladies' Clothing, which made it a bit embarrassing. It meant I had to stand next to all the underwear and stuff like that. I tried not to look at anything in case anyone saw me and thought I was staring or something.

'Huh huh huh! Buying your girlfriend some knickers?'

I jumped a mile! I almost hit the ceiling. I spun round and found myself gazing into Charlie Smugg's big, ugly chops. My own face was burning up.

'No!' I said, so loudly that everyone around me turned to stare and I went even redder.

Charlie looked at the audience and smiled. 'It's all right,' he explained. 'He can't remember what size pants his girlfriend wears.'

'Shut up!'

'Only trying to help,' sniggered Charlie.

'Just leave me alone.'

Charlie gave another shark-like smile. 'I've got plans for you,' he said. 'You and your girly-friend. You're going in that trough this time, and you're going to get filthy, big time. You're going to stink for the rest of your life.'

I shook my head. 'Streaker's going to beat your dogs.'

'Oh I don't think so,' crowed Charlie. 'She might beat one of them, but she won't beat all three, no way.' He poked my chest with a stubby, dirty finger. 'You're history, sunshine.'

'Yeah?' I bravely replied. 'Well if I'm history then you're . . . you're school dinners!'

That shut him up. It shut me up, too! I don't think either of us had any idea what I was on about.

Charlie just stared at me. Then he began shaking his head and finally he wandered off.

Everyone seemed to be looking at me now, but as soon as I stared back at them they hastily looked away. I turned back to the jewellery carousel. All I wanted to do now was get out of the shop as quickly as possible. I found a neat little bracelet with a heart dangling on it. I reckoned Melinda would love that. It looked just like gold, although of course it wasn't. I took it to the counter, paid and made a beeline for the door.

As I reached the outside I breathed a sigh of relief. Fresh air at last. I could get away from all those nosy faces. I began to relax and then suddenly an iron hand gripped my shoulder.

'Excuse me, young man.' A security guard held me in his vice-like grasp. 'I don't believe you've paid for that.'

'W-What?' I held up my little bag. 'I've g-g-got the receipt,' I stammered. 'I've only just bought it. There must be some mistake.'

'I don't think so, sonny. I don't mean what you have in the bag. I mean – this!' The guard reached behind my back and produced a flame-red bra-and-panties set.

I almost died on the spot. Everyone in the street had turned to stare. The guard kept waving this awful red set of underwear in my face, which was rapidly turning even redder than the knickers.

'But I don't know anything about them! I mean, why, what, where –?' I was gobsmacked. I couldn't think what to say. What was going on?

'You'll have to come with me,' insisted the

guard. 'I'm arresting you on suspicion of shoplifting.'

Before I knew it I was down at the police station and you can guess who was standing behind the front desk when I was dragged in.

Sergeant Smugg, Charlie's dad.

8 You Can Trust Freckles

It was only when I saw Sergeant Smugg that I began to put two and two together. Of course, Charlie Smugg, it had to be Charlie! He had been there in the shop, hovering around me. It was Charlie up to his tricks. He would have thought that was so funny.

'Well, well, well,' sneered Sergeant Smugg. 'If it isn't our old friend Trevor Larkey.' He nodded at the security guard. 'I know this lad. He's always in trouble. Didn't have a dog with him, did he? Partners in crime, they are.'

The guard shook his head. 'Didn't see any dog.'

'Hmmm. Could be that while you had your eyes on this lad the dog was making off with a shopload of goods.'

My jaw just about
hit the ground.
This was crazy!
Now Sergeant
Smugg seemed
to think that
Streaker had
gone whizzing out
of the shop with the
rest of the ladies underwear department! He
leaned right across the desk and pushed his fat
face up against mine.

'Who were you stealing this for? Not yourself,
obviously, ha ha ha! Maybe it was for your
mother?'

'I didn't steal them!'

'But the guard found you with them.'

'I didn't know I had it. It was stuck to my back.'

'Ha! "I didn't know I had it." That's what they
all say.' Sergeant Smugg put on a mocking voice.
'Stealing for your girlfriend maybe?' The police-

man eyed the guard again. 'Goes around with a girl. They work as a pair. They're both in it up to their necks, mark my words. If the dog wasn't there then the girl must have been. I could order a police raid on her house. We'll probably find it full of stolen goods.'

'I was on my own and I didn't steal them,' I repeated.

'Oh. So how did they get there then?'

'I don't know,' I answered miserably, although I was pretty sure. But could I tell the sergeant that his son had put them there? Would he believe me? Of course not. I stayed silent. Sergeant Smugg picked up the phone and dialled my home.

'We'll see what your father has to say about this,' he grunted.

Dad was not impressed to find himself called out to the police station. He didn't think much of me and he didn't think much of Sergeant Smugg either. 'Call yourself a policeman? Do you really think a young boy – or anyone for that matter – would deliberately walk out of a shop with a bra and panties hanging from their back? Even the guard says it looked odd. Someone obviously put them there for a prank.'

The guard from the department store nodded. 'I think Mr Larkey could be right. It did look strange. Usually shoplifters try and hide what they're stealing.'

'Exactly,' said Dad. 'Someone is talking sense at last. Perhaps you could also explain to me, Sergeant Smugg, why my eleven-year-old son would want to steal a flame-red bra and knick-ers?'

The sergeant picked up the underwear set and examined them. 'They are very flashy,' he suggested.

'Not for an eleven-year-old boy! And why on earth would he hang them from his back where everyone could see them?'

'Good point,' muttered the security guard.

'Yes, and it's a pity you didn't think of that

before bringing Trevor down here and wasting everyone's time,' snapped Dad.

'Sorry,' muttered the guard. 'I just got caught up in all the excitement. It's my first week on the job and I've never arrested anyone before.'

Sergeant Smugg shuffled a big pile of papers. 'Well you be careful,' he said eventually, throwing a big frown in my direction. 'I've got my eye on you. You get into too much trouble by far and I'll have you one day, I will. I'll have you and that'll be it. You and your dog. And that girl. And your father!'

Dad took me home and I told him I was sure it was Charlie. Dad gritted his teeth.

'It's war,' he said. 'I'm fed up with those Smuggs.'

Then he had a go at me. I told him it wasn't my fault. I hadn't arrested myself or taken myself to the police station. So then I got told off for being cheeky. You can't win, can you? As for Mum, when Dad told her the full story she fell off her exer-cycle laughing. I pointed out that it was her fault really.

'If it hadn't been for you I wouldn't have been in the shop in the first place.' I explained about the bracelet and they were impressed.

'It's lovely,' said Dad, rather surprised. 'Very romantic. I'm sure Tina will be yours forever.'

'Tina?!' Mum and I chorused.

Dad looked puzzled. 'Am I missing something?'

'It's for Melinda,' Mum told him.

'What? You mean Melinda as in Melinda Boffington-Orr with the designer jeans and top that have just cost us an arm and a leg to get cleaned? That Melinda? Boy, you do like living dangerously, don't you, Trevor?'

'How do you mean?' I asked.

Mum and Dad glanced at each other. 'You'll find out one day,' sighed Dad. 'And when it happens just think of it as a learning experience. In the meantime take that wretched dog out for a walk before she eats the entire carpet.'

I hate it when they say things like that. They almost tell you something that is obviously highly important and then they leave you in the dark. Still, I wasn't going to spend all day fretting about it. I took Streaker up to the field, let her off the lead and sat down under a tree to see if Melinda would turn up. While I waited I got out the bracelet and looked at it again. It sparkled in the sunshine and the tiny heart looked really cute. Melinda was going to love it. I carefully put it back in the tissue wrapping and slipped it into my pocket.

It wasn't long before a boxer came wandering over and started dribbling on my trainers. It was Roxy, and that meant Melinda was near by. I stood up and saw her just a short distance across the field. The sun was shining on her long hair. She looked stunning.

'Roxy! Where are you?'

'She's with me,' I said. 'Over here.'

Melinda shaded her eyes and looked across.

'Oh,' she said. 'It's you.' She began walking towards me. My hand went into my pocket and clutched the tissue. 'I suppose your dog is out here somewhere, terrorizing everyone,' she said.

I smiled a bit stupidly. 'Yes, well I'm sorry about what happened the other day.' There was a bit of a silence. 'Nice day,' I said. 'Sun's shining.' She was wearing a dazzling white T-shirt that made her skin looked tanned and lovely. I could see faint freckles across her nose.

'Freckles are nice,' I said.

'What?'

'My dad says you can always trust someone with freckles.'

I felt myself redden. What was I gabbling about? My dad had never said anything like that in his life! And it all sounded so stupid. It was like telling her pimples were nice, or athlete's foot. Stupid, stupid, stupid.

Melinda lifted one arm to look at her watch. It jangled. I stared at her arm. She was wearing a bracelet of heavy, solid gold. I could tell just by the look of it. A big chunky heart dangled from it, making a jingly noise every time her arm moved. I had never seen such a massive bracelet. I slipped my hand out of my pocket, empty.

'Nice bracelet,' I said.

'Daddy got it for me. It's solid gold. Someone else gave me the heart.' She blushed slightly. 'A

boy. Charlie. Maybe you know him?'

'Yeah,' I sighed. 'Oh well, got to go – Streaker's eating someone's leg. Bye.'

I walked away fast. My feet thumped into the ground and with every step I inwardly cursed Charlie Smugg.

To make matters worse I happened to pass the horse trough on my way back. What a foul, stinking, stagnant mess! It was fuller than it had been before too, which was odd because it hadn't rained that much. I remembered what Charlie had done the last time he had tried to get us in

the trough. He'd put in extra slime – great gloopy gobbets of the most revolting oily slop imaginable.

Charlie had obviously been at it again. He'd been sneaking out to the field and topping up the trough. I held a hand over my mouth and nose as I gazed into the stinking, bubbling gunge. At one end a large yellow grimy slick was slowly slithering across the surface, like some alien slime-monster from Planet Yukk.

This was the charming bath that Charlie was preparing for Tina and myself. Great.

9 In Trouble Again

I told Tina that Melinda was putting Roxy up for Best in Show. She shrugged and said that Melinda could do what she liked.

'She's going out with Charlie Smugg,' I added.

Tina smiled. 'I hope they'll be very happy together.' She clapped a hand to her mouth. 'Oh, Trev! I'm so sorry! I forgot, I mean, oh – whoops!'

'What do you mean – whoops?'

'Well, you and Melinda – you fancied her, didn't you?'

I felt the red rising up my face and I was very uncomfortable. Streaker bounced round my feet, trying to trip me up. That didn't help either.

'I'm so sorry,' Tina repeated. 'You must be devastated. Charlie Smugg, too – that's terrible.'

I tried to change the subject. 'Charlie's been topping up the trough like he did last time.'

'Why doesn't that surprise me?' mused Tina. 'He's a cheat through and through. I'm amazed that anyone sensible or nice would want to go out with the likes of him.'

'Let's concentrate on the dog show,' I said and I was even more embarrassed to find that my voice had gone croaky and I had difficulty trying to sound normal. 'We need to build an entire agility course this time so Streaker can get a good feel for it.'

We had reached the old football ground. Tina was examining the tyres we'd left out for the slalom. 'Somebody else has been here,' she said. 'Look. Tyre tracks. Someone on a bike has been using the slalom.'

We looked around, but the place was deserted. 'They're not here now, whoever it was,' I pointed out and began dragging at a piece of filthy tarpaulin. 'Give me a hand with this. We can make a tunnel.'

While Tina and I struggled with the tarpaulin Streaker galloped up and down, chasing flies, throwing herself at the tyres and leaping on to ancient vehicles. If only the agility course had derelict burned-out cars in it, and abandoned fridges, Streaker would win easily. She was brilliant. She flew about the place like some manic stunt dog.

'I've never seen a dog with so much energy,' Tina observed, as Streaker hurled herself from the roof of a truck, landed on a mattress, rolled off, seized a tyre and bit it to death. 'She's got more energy than a power station.'

'Yeah, we should hook her up to the National Grid. Streaker could produce enough electricity to boil a million kettles.'

'You're madder than she is,' Tina grinned.

We pushed some old tumble-drier carcasses close to each other, leaving a channel between them. Then we draped the tarpaulin over the top and let it flop over the sides. Tina crouched down and peered through from one end to the other. 'Just like the real thing,' she said. 'You get Streaker and set her off from the other end.'

'*You get Streaker.*' That's what Tina said. Her exact words. Ha ha ha. Very funny. I tried the 'Walkies' trick but Streaker had gone deaf. You try catching a dog that can run at a hundred miles an hour, perform more stunts than James Bond and has no idea what 'SIT!' means. It took me ten minutes to get her, and by the time I had finished I was covered in dirt of all varieties.

I held Streaker down at one end of the tunnel while Tina called from the other. 'And don't ask me to make squirrel noises this time,' she yelled.

'Can you do a rabbit?' I yelled back.

Tina frowned and vanished below the top of the tunnel. I peered down the dark tube. I could see her at the other end. She had both hands stuck above her head and was waggling them like ears. 'Weeweeweeweeweeweeweeweewee.' She wiggled her nose.

'That's not a rabbit,' I told her. 'That's this little piggy going weewee all the way home.'

'Can you do any better?'

I let Streaker go and began to hop round my end of the tunnel. 'Bloop!' I said. 'Bloopbloopbloop!' Streaker wasn't the least bit interested and wandered away.

'Rabbits don't say "*bloop*",' Tina shouted from the far end.

'They don't go "weeweewee" either,' I answered back.

'What do they say then?'

'Oh, I don't know. Be something else.'

But it wasn't necessary because Streaker suddenly came charging up and zoomed straight down the tunnel like a rocket. Whoosh!

'Brilliant!' I yelled and was instantly knocked flying by an Alsatian that came tearing after her. I hardly had time to realize what was happening when two more Alsatians thundered past, knocking my feet from under me so that I landed heavily on my backside.

There was a yell from the other end of the tunnel as Streaker whizzed between Tina's legs and then she too was bowled over by the Alsatians and away the dogs went, in a cloud of dust. This was quickly followed by a thunderous

roar and we saw a scrambler bike bouncing across the old pitch towards us, dodging between all the bits of scattered rubbish. Charlie Smugg – who else could it be?

But there was something odd. There were two – no, THREE people on the bike! One was riding it and the other two appeared to be standing with one foot on the back seat, clasping each other with one arm while sticking out their free arm and leg in mid-air like some circus act.

The bike juddered to a halt by the tunnel and the two acrobats pulled off their helmets, still balancing on the back seat in a very showing-off kind of way. Sergeant Smugg and Charlie. And the rider was . . .?

The police superintendent himself. Boris Boffington-Orr the Great. Boris the Black Belt Tae Kwon Do. Boris the Blue Peter Badge Holder (Twice).

'I might have known,' snarled Sergeant Smugg. 'Trespassers. This place is out of bounds. It would be you two, wouldn't it?' He turned to his chief. 'These two are known troublemakers. What are you doing here?'

'What are *you* doing here?' asked Tina, innocently.

'Keeping an eye out for vandals like you.'

The pack of charging dogs reached the furthest end of the old football pitch. Streaker performed a stunningly tight handbrake turn and came hurtling back towards us. The Smuggs' three Alsatians tried a similar manoeuvre, lost their grip, crashed into each other, went sprawling in the dirt, scrambled to their feet and set off after Streaker once again.

'It is forbidden for the general public to enter this place,' Sergeant Smugg continued, sticking out his belly in a bid to look even more important.

The dogs were getting closer . . .

'Are you on duty?' asked Tina.

'A policeman never sleeps,' said B-O.

. . . and closer . . .

'It looked to me as if you were playing on your bike,' Tina said.

'Do you know to whom you're speaking?' snarled B-O.

. . . and closer still. Maybe I should say something?

And at that point Streaker arrived.

Now then, you have to get the right picture. Streaker was being chased by three Alsatians, each one three times her size and weight. She was travelling at full speed. To get some idea of how fast this was, think of any number above zero.

Now multiply it by five. Add fifty. Add a hundred. Multiply by ten. Now add a thousand and you have the speed at which Streaker was travelling – although it might actually have been a trifle faster – depends what number you started with.

So, Streaker arrives like a cruise missile fitted with booster rockets. She leaps! Oh! You should have seen it! Such a glorious leap! Like an antelope! No, I'm getting muddled now. She can't be a cruise missile *and* an antelope. OK, you'll just have to imagine an antelope with a cruise missile strapped to her back – and fitted with booster rockets. Back to what happened . . .

. . . Streaker leaps, way into the air! Right over their heads she flies like a soaring albatross. (An albatross clutching a cruise missile strapped to an antelope, etc., etc.)

'Oh-woh!' cry Sergeant Smugg and Charlie and Boff-a-lot as Streaker zooms right over them.

And then the three Alsatians arrive. Each one is three times bigger than Streaker. Each one weighs three times more than Streaker. They arrive at full speed. They leap. Like antelopes? No. They soar like albatrosses? No.

The three Alsatians leap like rhinoceroses.

Have you ever seen a rhinoceros leap?

No. Of course you haven't.

And why not?

Because they can't. Rhinoceroses can do three things. They can go. They can stop and they can crash into things. And that is what the Smuggs' Alsatians did. They smashed straight into the bikers themselves, so it was not just the dogs that crashed. It was Charlie, his dad, Boffington-Orr and the scrambler bike, all at the same time. There was a walloping collision and the bike went over. All three were thrown to the ground.

They had dogs on top of them and dogs beneath them. One Alsatian was not at all pleased to find the superintendent sitting on his back legs, so he bit Boffington-Orr's bottom.

'Aaargh!'

Well, at least that got the superintendent back on his feet pretty quickly. He was furious. And that's how Tina and I both ended up at the police station, under arrest.

10 A Bit of Progress at Last

Dad was not very pleased. 'I'm fed up with coming down here because you've arrested my son,' he told Sergeant Smugg.

'Don't forget the dog,' the policeman sneered. 'I've arrested your dog, too.'

'Oh, for heaven's sake! What's she done this time?'

'She attacked me.'

'She did not! It's not true, Dad!' I shouted. 'All she did was jump right over him. You should have seen her!'

'Trevor's right, Mr Larkey,' Tina butted in. 'Streaker was being chased by three Alsatians and she leaped over them. The Alsatians tried to follow but they knocked over Sergeant Smugg,

Charlie and Mr Boffington-Orr instead.'

Dad swallowed and glanced nervously round the office. 'Mr Boffington-Orr was there, too? Where is he now?'

'The superintendent is being attended to,' growled Sergeant Smugg.

'One of the dogs bit his bottom,' I put in.

Dad choked, coughed, spluttered and desperately tried to keep a straight face. 'Oh dear,' he squeaked. 'Was it a bad bite?'

'The super hasn't allowed anyone except the doctor to take a look,' Sergeant Smugg answered, a trifle coldly. 'However, the superintendent has asked me to inform you that as a result of today's incident your dog is now on the Dangerous Animals Register, and if your dog does not show some progress in the forthcoming show then she will have to be put down.'

'WHAT??!!'

'Dad?' I croaked, almost speechless.

'You can't do this,' Dad growled, shaking his head.

'Your dog bit the police superintendent,' Smugg began but he was shouted down by Tina and myself.

'That was one of your Alsatians!'

Smugg shook his head and smiled. 'Oh I don't think so. The superintendent and I both know what really happened.'

'Dad! Dad! It wasn't Streaker! It wasn't!' I was beside myself, almost crying.

'This is gross injustice,' shouted Dad. 'You can't do it.'

'I'm not doing it. It's a direct order from the police superintendent,' Sergeant Smugg replied evenly.

'Don't think you can hide behind him,' snarled Dad. 'You're enjoying this, aren't you?'

'Your dog's a menace,' Smugg snarled back.

'And a police order is a police order. Good day to you all, and don't let me catch you at the old football ground again.'

We were silent going home in the car. The awfulness of it all was really sinking in now. Tina and I sat in the back. Her hand was on the seat, almost touching me and I so wanted to hold it tight.

I couldn't do it. What if she pulled her hand away? She might even scream. So I didn't hold her hand, didn't even look at her, and I felt so, so miserable.

Dad quietly asked how Streaker's training was coming on. Would she be all right in the agility test? Boffington-Orr was really breathing down our necks now. I told him how brilliant Streaker was at jumping and running, twisting and turning.

'But will she complete the agility test?' Dad repeated. 'Will she beat those wretched Alsatians?'

'All we have to do is get her to jump and twist at the right time,' explained Tina.

'Is that a "yes" or a "no"?' asked Dad.

'It's . . . a maybe,' Tina offered, always trying to be positive.

Dad gave a long sigh, and Mum pointed out that we only had two days left before the dog show. Gulp.

Tina and I sat in the back garden and talked things through. She couldn't understand why the Smuggs had been at the football ground anyway. I told her what Charlie had said about the police motorbike display team.

'They must have been practising for that.'

'I guess that means we can't go back to the football ground then,' Tina murmured. 'Streaker will just have to do the best she can on the day.'

'But she's hopeless, Tina! OK, she can do the Wall of Death, as long as you pretend to be a squirrel. She might go through the tunnel if she feels like it. Heaven knows what she'll make of the slalom and we haven't even tried the hoop or the see-saw with her.'

Tina jumped up. 'We can do the see-saw here, in the garden. It's only a plank balancing on an old oil drum or something. The dog walks up one end until the other end goes down and then she walks along and gets off. Simple.'

Tina made it sound really easy so I hunted out a long plank of wood. Then we found a small trestle that Dad used for sawing things sometimes. We balanced the plank so one end was on the ground and the other in the air.

I went and fetched Streaker and held her at one end of the see-saw. 'Come on. Good dog. Walk the plank!' Streaker looked at me, stuck out her long tongue and took a long slurp at my nose as if it were an ice cream. 'No – just walk up here. Come on.'

Tina stood at the other end and called her. Streaker look at Tina, pricked up her ears, trotted up the plank, the see-saw tipped, down went

Streaker and off she got. I was gobsmacked.

'You did it!' cried Tina, hugging Streaker. 'Well done! Clever dog!'

'Quick, try it again from your end,' I said.

Tina took Streaker to the see-saw. I called her. Up she trotted, down went the see-saw and off she got. She turned about and did it again, and again and again. Fantastic.

'She likes it,' I shouted. 'She actually likes doing it.'

Tina grinned across at me. 'That just leaves the hoop.'

'The hoop's like the tunnel really,' I pointed out.

'How do you mean?'

'Well, you go through a hoop and you go through a tunnel. The difference is that a tunnel is much, much longer than a hoop. A hoop is like a very small bit of a tunnel, as if someone has got a tunnel and sliced off a teeny-weeny sliver of it and called that bit a hoop.'

'You're mad,' Tina laughed.

'I'm just saying that if Streaker will go through a tunnel she won't mind going through a hoop.'

'But she has to jump through it.'

'Oh yes, I forgot about that bit. Tell you what – there's an old window frame in the shed. We could use that.'

I ran to the shed and hoiked out a rather cob-webby window frame. It didn't have any glass in it. 'There.'

'But it's rectangular. Hoops are circular.'

'Think of it as a square hoop,' I suggested.

'You are definitely mad.'

'It's all we've got,' I answered, and I held it up. Would Streaker jump through it? She ran round it. She barked at it. She jumped through my legs. She went up and down the see-saw, seven times, and then, just as I was about to give up – wheeee! She sailed through the frame. At last there was a very faint ray of hope. Tina and I looked at each other and grinned.

'Sorted,' she said.

'Sorted,' I echoed. 'Apart from the slalom.'

11 B-O Makes His Move

The arena was heaving with people, and backstage was even worse. It was not just full of
nervous, jumpy, over-excited dogs, it was stuffed
with nervous jumpy over-excited dog owners too,
all rushing about. The noise! It was like being
shut inside a dustbin with twenty dogs and an
incredibly loud echo.

Tina was wandering about looking very
excited, searching for Charlie Smugg of all
people. 'Have you heard? Roxy's been withdrawn
from the competition! She's got a flea infestation
and the vet won't let her take part!'

This was the first bit of really good news I'd
heard for ages. 'Hurrah. Wonder where she got
them from?'

'Charlie probably,' she joked. 'He must be around here somewhere.'

'What do you want him for?'

'I don't. I want to know where his dog is. You know they've entered all three Alsatians – one for Obedience, one for Agility and one for Best Groomed. Have you seen the competition for Best Groomed? Mouse doesn't have a chance. Anyhow, I've got some very special super-duper shampoo here. I thought Charlie might like it.'

I was flabbergasted. 'Why on earth are you helping Charlie?'

Tina smiled. 'I'll explain later. Look, there he is. He's just about to give the dog a last wash. Distract him for two seconds, will you?'

'Why?'

'Don't you ever stop asking questions? Just do it!'

By this time we were closing in. Charlie was running some warm water into a big plastic tub. I went and stood next to him.

'You'll never get him clean,' I teased.

'What? Oh, it's you. I might have known. Don't think you can wind me up because you're dead, mate. Your dog's going down and that'll be the end of her. Ha!' Charlie drew a finger across his throat, like he was cutting it. He had a huge, sneering grin plastered across his face. Evil was the only word to describe him.

He stood there crowing and behind him, unseen, Tina fiddled with the dog-cleaning stuff. I hadn't got a clue what she was doing but she silently slipped away and I guessed she must have done what she needed.

'Streaker pulled off a big surprise once before,' I said boldly. 'She can do it again, too. You wait and see.'

And I hurried off, wishing that I had convinced myself by what I'd just said to Charlie. I hadn't of course. Tina and I might just as well all go and climb into the horse trough right away. Why wait for the dog show and the shame and embarrassment it was about to heap on our heads? And as for poor Streaker . . .

The agility trial was going to be the last event because it involved so many different things. The show started with the obedience test and Sergeant Smugg was on top form. You should have seen him! His chest was all puffed out – you'd have thought it was him on show, not his dog.

He marched up and down. The dog marched up and down. He blew whistles, he shouted orders and the dog came and went and fetched and sat and jumped and lay down and stood and did exactly what he was supposed to. He got through to the last stage without gaining a single penalty. The last test was when one of the judges approached the dogs and held out a hand. Each dog was supposed to place a paw in the judge's hand so that they could shake. It was a nice, silly end to the display.

Well, along came the judge, stood in front of Sergeant Smugg's Alsatian and held out a hand.

The dog leaned forwards and grabbed the hand
in his jaw. He wouldn't let go. The judge
squirmed in pain and Sergeant Smugg went very
red.

'He thinks you're a burglar,' explained the
policeman.

'I'm not! Tell him I'm not!'

'I can't speak dog,' muttered the sergeant and

the crowd started to laugh. 'I've never had to tell him that before because once he's got a burglar he's trained not to let go.'

The crowd guffawed.

'Get him off me! He's hurting!'

But the dog growled and snarled and gripped the hand harder. Eventually all three had to leave the arena together. Not surprisingly Sergeant Smugg's Number One Alsatian was disqualified. The winner was Ruby, a Border Collie. (Real name: Hildebrand Ginwallah McDougall X. Blimey!) But the important thing was that having been disqualified, Number One Alsatian was automatically banned from taking part in any further events – in other words it was one less Alsatian for Streaker to beat.

Number Two Alsatian was entered for Best Groomed, along with Mouse and several more. The dogs shone and sparkled as if they'd just been put through a car wash several times, which was pretty close to the truth I suppose.

One by one they were called out and paraded in front of the crowd. They were stunning.

'The next entrant is Mouse, a St Bernard,' intoned a judge and Tina appeared.

I couldn't believe my eyes. Mouse was totally splendid, as neat and tidy as if he'd been at the hairdresser's salon for a whole week. He was obviously enjoying his moment of glory and trotted with paws lifted high and his coat sparkling. He was wonderful. I clapped and cheered myself hoarse.

'And the final entrant is from Charlie Smugg with his Alsatian, Number Two.'

There was a long pause. All eyes were fixed on the entry tunnel but there was no sign of movement.

'Would Charlie Smugg please bring his dog into the arena?'

Another pause. What was going on? There came a gasp from the crowd as Charlie first stuck his head round the corner and then walked in, slowly – very slowly. He sort of sidled in, keeping to the very edge of the arena, as if he didn't wish to be seen. He pulled on the dog lead and at the other end appeared . . .

. . . a dog? Was it really a dog? It certainly had four legs. But it was the weirdest creature I had ever seen. It was part green, part black, part brown, part red. The wet bits were all soggy and sloppy. The dry bits stuck up in thick, sticky clumps. The tail drooped between the legs and trailed on the ground. It was the most filthy, yukkiest, scum-ridden stinkpot of a dog you were ever likely to see. The crowd clearly thought some kind of joke was taking place because they began laughing and pointing and chuckling.

Charlie scowled back and told the judge that he'd had an accident with the shampoo. 'I think it had gone off,' he said.

'Oh dear,' murmured the judge, holding her nose. 'Yes, it is rather smelly, isn't it? Would you mind awfully just taking it away and giving it a good bath?'

So guess who the winner was? Mouse! Brilliant! I was so pleased for Tina and amazed that so far the two Alsatians had not gained a single point. I also had a sneaking suspicion that Tina might have had something to do with the appearance of Charlie's stink bomb on legs.

'All I did was give him a different shampoo,' she whispered, all wide-eyed innocence.

'It was foul! Where did it come from? It looked just like that revolting stuff in the . . .' The penny dropped. 'Tina! You never . . .?' She nodded and grinned madly.

'Contestants for the agility trials please prepare your dogs,' went the speakers. My heart instantly began beating wildly. This was it. The Moment of Truth. I raced backstage to collect Streaker. And that was when I saw the note. It was pinned to Streaker's cage, where it fluttered slightly in the draught.

This dog has been disqualified from taking part
because of a restraining order placed upon it.
By Order of B. Boffington-Orr, Police Superintendent.
S.W.G. (Chairman) T.K.D.
(Black Belt) B.P.B.H. (Twice)

How could he do that? Why? What was going on?

Tina caught up with me, still buzzing with excitement from winning Best Groomed. She read the note and her jaw just about hit the ground.

'He can't do that! He's just trying to get out of it!'

'Get out of what?' I asked tiredly. I stared at the note, reading it over and over again. Only moments before I had felt like a hot-air balloon in full, glorious flight. Now all the air was gone and I was just a flabby, useless heap.

'Don't you understand anything, Trev? There's only the agility test to go and B-O can't afford to let Streaker have any chance of doing

better than the Smugg Alsatians. He doesn't want to lose face. He's scared, so he's trying to disqualify Streaker.'

Streaker gave a short bark and stuck out her tongue. That was how I felt about it too. I was angry and I was worried. I stared at the note, scouring my brain for an answer, but the more I searched the less I saw.

'Not much we can do about it, is there? You can't overrule the police superintendent. Streaker's out of the show and that's final. That means we lose big time.'

I don't think I have ever seen Tina looking so dangerously angry. She punched my arm, hard.

'Ow!'

'You give up so easily, Trev. I've no idea why I want to go out with you.'

'Out with me?' I protested. 'What are you on about?'

But we were interrupted by the arrival of Boffington-Orr himself. He was walking rather stiffly, as if his backside was giving him some pain, which pleased me since he was such a pain in the backside himself. Even so he flashed a huge smile at the pair of us.

'So sorry about your dog,' he smirked. 'But it had to be done. Can't have dogs biting police officers, can we? I did it for everyone's safety.

Shame she can't take part.'

'But Streaker didn't bite you!' I cried. 'It was one of Sergeant Smugg's Alsatians!'

'Oh no, I don't think so,' said B-O, still smiling and shaking his head. 'Not a policeman's dog. Oh no. A policeman's dog wouldn't do that.'

'One of Sergeant Smugg's dogs has just bitten a judge,' Tina pointed out icily.

'A simple mistake. Anyhow, I'm afraid the order has been made and that's that.'

'You can't do this!' I yelled. 'It's not fair! It wasn't Streaker!'

'Prove it,' chuckled the Chief of Police. 'Go on, prove it.'

I was stunned. I just couldn't think what to say. B-O knew it wasn't Streaker. He knew! Tina seemed pretty gobsmacked, too. An announcement crackled through the loudspeakers.

'Would the owner of Mouse please report to the arena, where the prize-giving for Best-Groomed Dog will now take place.'

'You'd better go,' I muttered. 'You mustn't miss that. Go on, quick!'

Tina didn't want to leave things as they were, but the announcement came again and she ran off, almost in tears. I turned back to Streaker. She looked at me with her usual daft, lopsided grin. She had no idea that the sky had just fallen in on top of all of us.

12 Show Time!

I sank down to the ground, with my back against Streaker's stand, and watched as B-O sauntered stiffly away. My brain was numb. I was only vaguely aware of the noises from the arena, broadcast behind the scenes by the speaker system. The trophies for Best-Groomed Dog were being presented. There were cheers for third and second place and of course an enormous one for the winner, Tina.

I felt ridiculously pleased and proud of her. At least Mouse had done something brilliant, but only because Tina had got her so well groomed. Tina was thanking the judges for the trophy.

'It's fantastic – almost the best day in my life,' she said over the speakers. 'But not quite, because right at this moment, backstage, a dreadful mis-carriage of justice is going on. A dog back there, Streaker, has been disqualified from the agility trial for biting the police superintendent. I know, because I was there, that it was not Streaker that bit the Super. It was a policeman's dog that did it – one of Sergeant Smugg's Alsatians.'

There was a snigger or two from the crowd, but Tina calmly continued.

'Mr Boffington-Orr has told me to prove it. Well, I can. Streaker is a lot smaller than a police Alsatian. Her jaw is narrower and her teeth are closer together. If there is a vet here all we have to do is measure Streaker's bite and compare it to the teethmarks on Mr Boffington-Orr's bottom.'

The audience just hooted. They thought it was so funny, and brave of Tina to speak out. They began shouting for a vet and soon one made himself known. They called for the super-intendent and there was nothing he could do about it. He went to a private spot with the vet. Then there was a long wait as various measurements were made and, well, you've probably

guessed what happened. Streaker was cleared! B-O could not do anything except admit that he'd been wrong and that it was a police dog that had bitten him.

The crowd yelled. They went mad. Backstage, I was going mad, too! I grabbed Streaker and the agility trials began.

Streaker did better than I thought. She whizzed up and down that see-saw. She flew through the hoop and the tunnel. OK, so she flew through both of them the wrong way round and got some penalty points, but I was pretty amazed that she'd negotiated them at all. She stopped dead at the Wall of Death and it wasn't until Tina started making squirrel noises from the side of the arena that Streaker finally got the message and went up in one gigantic leap. The crowd cheered at that point and I felt pretty good. They obviously liked a dog that tried hard.

Then came the slalom. Oh dear. Eight traffic cones stood in a straight line, and all Streaker had to do was weave between them. Well, you remember what happened the first time Streaker practised this, back at the old football ground, with the tyres that Tina and I had put out for her. Do you remember what she did?

This was more or less a repeat performance. Streaker raced for the first cone, knocked it flying, chased it around for a while and bit it a few times. She did the same to the second cone. She jumped on the third cone and squashed it flat. She tried to head the fourth into an imaginary goal. She widdled on the fifth, which sent the crowd into hysterics and then sat down and washed herself. Game over.

I can't remember how many penalty points she got for that, and anyhow I hardly had time to think about it because the next contestant was Sergeant Smugg with Alsatian Number Three.

That dog was perfect. He was a policeman's dog, highly trained, and boy, did it show! He ran and trotted and jumped as if he had done nothing else for years.

He didn't pick up a single penalty point. I stood at the side of the ring with Streaker and the other contestants and I watched this faultless performance and my heart sank and sank and sank, deep into that horse trough. There was no way Tina and I were going to avoid it now. Smugg and Boffy the Mongrel Slayer had won.

Alsatian Number Three only had the slalom left to do.

Sergeant Smugg slipped his hand from the dog's collar and off he went, whizzing round each cone in perfect style. One cone, two, three, four, five and then, suddenly, the dog skidded to a halt. He trotted back to the fifth cone and began sniffing suspiciously all round it.

It was the one Streaker had peed on. You know what dogs are like! Number Three sniffed and sniffed and paced round and round and then, blow me down, cocked his leg and did a walloping wee right on top of Streaker's! The crowd started laughing again, but instead of carrying on with the test Number Three was now staring around the arena. He knew Streaker was there somewhere. They spotted each other and the Alsatian was off like a rocket again, heading straight for Streaker, barking furiously.

Streaker wasn't going to hang around when there was an Alsatian tank chasing her. By this time of course you know that Streaker can run fast – very fast. And she can turn corners like a born rally driver. She just flew round that arena, with the Alsatian in hot pursuit – through the tunnel, over the wall, round the cones, up and down the see-saw, and every time they went round a few more dogs joined in.

In a matter of seconds the entire arena appeared to be boiling over with dogs, barking and yapping and chasing each other, themselves, their owners, the judges. Several leaped into the front rows and sent people hastily clambering over each other for safety. There were a few bites here and there and a lot of loud yells and shouts

from the poor victims and, all in all, it was about twenty minutes before calm was restored.

The long and short of it was that Streaker had so many penalty points she came last. But Alsatian Number Three, who had caused all that trouble, was disqualified and led away in disgrace. Not only that but even as we were congratulating ourselves there was a further announcement, this time about the Police Motorcycle Display.

'Unfortunately, due to the indisposition of one

of the team, the display will not now take place.'
We burst out laughing. Indisposition? What they
really meant was that a certain somebody had a
very sore bum!

So Sergeant Smugg was not a happy man. But
I was, and so was my dad and so was Tina.
(Well, obviously Tina wasn't a happy man, but
you know what I mean.)

Charlie Smugg had lost that bet. B-O had been
beaten. I could hardly believe it. Tina and I were

over the moon, even though we knew that there was no way we would get Charlie anywhere near the horse trough, let alone into it. We were just happy that we didn't have to take that gruesome bath ourselves. And the most brilliant thing of all was that Streaker was saved! Fantasti-funderful!

A few days after the dog-show fiasco we saw Charlie up in the field, walking with Melinda, Roxy and the three Alsatians. They made a right little gang and as soon as the dogs saw Streaker they came after her. Streaker immediately set off at breakneck speed in the opposite direction. Charlie chuckled with pleasure as he watched four, big, snapping, yapping monsters pound after her.

'Shame about the dog show,' Tina said, all innocence. 'You going to get in the tub then?'

'No way. You gonna make me?' Charlie laughed. 'You only won because our dog was disqualified.' Melinda smiled and threaded her arm through his.

'Badly trained,' I said. 'If you need some help with training Tina and I are quite good at it.'

'Oh yeah, right,' sneered Charlie. 'You couldn't train a dead mouse!'

'Wanna bet?' I said.

Charlie didn't answer this time. (Thank goodness!)

We had reached the horse trough. It looked even more foul than before. Tina and I couldn't help sniggering, knowing what had gone into Charlie's dog shampoo.

'What are you two laughing at?' he demanded. 'You laughing at me?'

'Wouldn't dream of it, Charlie.'

He stared at us very suspiciously. In the distance I saw a pair of flapping ears approaching fast. I heard the telltale bark-bark-bark of three Alsatians. They were after Streaker again, with Roxy puffing and panting in fourth place, and the whole doggy hurricane was heading straight for us.

137

With a single cheerful yap Streaker took a flying leap – amazing – right over Charlie's head and down on the far side of the horse trough and away into the field again. Then the Alsatians arrived, one, two, three, all leaping after her.

'Hur, hur, hur,' laughed Charlie. 'They'll give your dog what-for when they get her,' he began, and then Roxy arrived. Roxy couldn't jump as well as the others. She tried the leap but missed. Instead she cannoned straight into Melinda. Melinda fell backwards, still clutching Charlie's arm. She stumbled against the trough behind her . . .

You get the picture, don't you? Go on, just picture it in your mind in full glorious Technicolor detail. Run it past your inner eyes in slo-mo. Roxy arrives – the big, beefy, chunky boxer, Wisteria Wannabee Winstanley VIII, her full weight flying into Melinda's chest. Melinda staggers back, stumbles against the lip of the trough and then she goes over, falling backwards, dragging Charlie with her. There's an almighty SPLASH and PHWIIIISH of water as three bodies tumble into the horse trough.

When they finally surface they are black from head to toe, and also brown, red, grey, green and soaked to the skin. Their clothes are filthy. Their skin is filthy, and boy, do they stink!

Charlie was almost speechless. Almost. 'You!' he bellowed.

'Wasn't us, Charlie,' Tina pointed out. 'It was Roxy.' And almost as if to prove it the three Alsatians arrived back and decided to join their owner in the delicious bath. One, two, three. Plip, plop, plap. Down beneath the surface went Charlie and Melinda again.

They surfaced, struggling for breath, slipping in the gunge, falling over each other, disappearing under the surface yet again. Melinda, who was unrecognizable by this stage, was howling her head off.

'My dad says you should never trust anyone

who needs three Alsatians,' I said.

Tina and I laughed all the way home. We
were still laughing when we reached my house.

'That was just so brilliant,' said Tina.

'Yeah, it was.' I looked at her. 'Thanks. None of it would have happened if it hadn't been for you.'

Tina blushed. 'It was both of us,' she protested.

'I know, that's what I mean. I couldn't have done it on my own. I'm sorry about Melinda and all that.'

'Oh, right.'

I felt in my pocket and brought out the little bracelet. 'It's to say "thank you",' I muttered. I felt weird – full of embarrassment and pride and hope and pleasure, all mixed up together so they made an uncomfortable feeling in my stomach. I dropped the bracelet into Tina's palm.

'For me?' she said, gazing down at the chain. She pushed it gently with one finger. 'It's beautiful,' she whispered. 'It's got a little heart on it.' She looked up at me with shining eyes. 'Is that your heart or mine?'

I bit my lip. 'Mine,' I said, in a faintly squeaky voice.

With regard to the unfortunate incident on
page 131,
Streaker would like to point out that not all
female dogs can do that,
but she can
because she's clever,
so there!

Log on and laugh for hours!

100-mile-an-hour amusement at the KRAZY KLUB

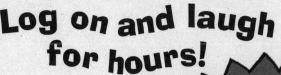

CRAVING MORE SILLINESS? Join Jeremy's KRAZY KLUB at jeremystrong.co.uk

Loaded with:
exclusive personal content straight from

Jeremy Strong

Fab **competitions**

Fun stuff

Sneaky **previews**

Interactive **polls**

Hot gossip

and lots more rib-tickling treats!

Ask Jeremy

Of all the books you have written, which one is your favourite?

I loved writing both **KRAZY KOW SAVES THE WORLD – WELL, ALMOST** and **STUFF**, my first book for teenagers. Both these made me laugh out loud while I was writing and I was pleased with the overall result in each case. I also love writing the stories about Nicholas and his daft family – **MY DAD**, **MY MUM**, **MY BROTHER** and so on.

If you couldn't be a writer what would you be?

Well, I'd be pretty fed up for a start, because writing was the one thing I knew I wanted to do from the age of nine onward. But if I DID have to do something else, I would love to be either an accomplished pianist or an artist of some sort. Music and art have played a big part in my whole life and I would love to be involved in them in some way.

What's the best thing about writing stories?

Oh dear – so many things to say here! Getting paid for making things up is pretty high on the list! It's also something you do on your own, inside your own head – nobody can interfere with that. The only boss you have is yourself. And you are creating something that nobody else has made before you. I also love making my readers laugh and want to read more and more.

Did you ever have a nightmare teacher? (And who was your best ever?)

My nightmare at primary school was Mrs Chappell, long since dead. I knew her secret – she was not actually human. She was a Tyrannosaurus rex in disguise. She taught me for two years when I was in Y5 and Y6, and we didn't like each other at all. My best ever was when I was in Y3 and Y4. Her name was Miss Cox, and she was the one who first encouraged me to write stories. She was brilliant. Sadly, she is long dead too.

When you were a kid you used to play kiss-chase. Did you always do the chasing or did anyone ever chase you?!

I usually did the chasing, but when I got chased, I didn't bother to run very fast! Maybe I shouldn't admit to that! We didn't play kiss-chase at school – it was usually played during holidays. If we had tried playing it at school we would have been in serious trouble. Mind you, I seemed to spend most of my time in trouble of one sort or another, so maybe it wouldn't have mattered that much.

14½ Things You Didn't Know About

Jeremy Strong

* * * * * * * * * * * * * * * * * *

1. He loves eating liquorice.

2. He used to like diving. He once dived from the high board and his trunks came off!

3. He used to play electric violin in a rock band called THE INEDIBLE CHEESE SANDWICH.

4. He got a 100-metre swimming certificate when he couldn't even swim.

5. When he was five, he sat on a heater and burnt his bottom.

6. Jeremy used to look after a dog that kept eating his underpants. (No – NOT while he was wearing them!)

7. When he was five, he left a basin tap running with the plug in and flooded the bathroom.

8. He can make his ears waggle.

9. He has visited over a thousand schools.

10. He once scored minus ten in an exam! That's ten less than nothing!

11. His hair has gone grey, but his mind hasn't.

12. He'd like to have a pet tiger.

13. He'd like to learn the piano.

14. He has dreadful handwriting.

And a half . . . His favourite hobby is sleeping. He's very good at it.

This is the first story about my crazy family. We're not all crazy of course – it's Dad mostly. I mean, who would think of bringing home an alligator as a pet? It got into our next-door neighbour's garden and ate all the fish from his pond. It even got into his car! That gave him quite a surprise, I can tell you! He was not very happy about it. Mum says Crunchbag will have to go, but Dad and I quite like him, even if his teeth are rather big and sharp.

LAUGH YOUR SOCKS OFF WITH

MY DAD'S GOT AN ALLIGATOR!

Available Now!

* * * * * * * * * * * * * * * * * *

Big problems in my family – we're running out of money fast. Dad reckons we should start up our own mini-farm. But the yoghurt we made exploded, and the goat needed an aromatherapy massage!

That's the sort of daft thing that happens in my family. And then my baby bro, Cheese (yes – I know Cheese is a very odd name for a baby!), was spotted on national television showing off his bottom!

LAUGH YOUR SOCKS OFF WITH

MY BROTHER'S FAMOUS BOTTOM

Available Now!

Psssst! Look what we overheard . . . What you really think about

Jeremy Strong . . .

Your mind is a basketful of ideas . . .

The pages really come to life

Your brain must always be on to have so many ideas

My pals just want to say that your books rule

We adore your books because they're hysterical!

Why do you wear strange belts?